Let's Play Tag!

📖 Read the Page

▶ Read the Story

🔄 Repeat

⏹ Stop

⭐ Game

⭐ Level 1   ⭐⭐ Level 2   ⭐⭐⭐ Level 3

💻

suey

cookies

soup

dumplings

PO'S TASTY TRAINING

written by Scott Sonneborn

illustrated by Clio Chiang

Po couldn't believe it. He had been chosen as the Dragon Warrior!

"Me?" said Po.

The crowd cheered.

Po was surprised. He wasn't very good at kung fu. The only thing he was good at was eating.

It didn't matter. He was going to train
with Master Shifu!

Shifu taught the best warriors in the land. Warriors like the Furious Five.

"I hope I can be as awesome as those guys one day," thought Po.

Po smiled as he watched the Furious Five train.

Master Shifu did not. Shifu was a tough teacher. No one could remember the last time he smiled.

Shifu looked at his new student and his frown grew even deeper.

"Look at your flabby arms!" said Shifu. "Your ridiculous belly! Your stinky breath!"

"Now wait a minute," said Po. "That's— owwwwww!"

"Quiet," said Shifu as he grabbed Po in a finger hold. It was time for his training to begin!

Po was nervous. The training equipment looked very scary. Then Po saw a friendly-looking training dummy in the corner.

"Maybe I can start with that," he said.

Po hit the dummy. It bounced back and smacked Po in the face.

"Yow!" cried Po.

WHACK!

WHACK!

Po bounced from one painful
piece of equipment to the next.

"Ooooooh!" moaned Po.

WHACK!

Shifu just shook his
head in disgust.

"I stink worse than anyone's ever stunk in the history of kung fu," said Po, sadly.

There was only one thing that could cheer him up. A cookie!

The cookies were on the top shelf. Po flipped in the air. He did a perfect kung fu split and grabbed a cookie.

That gave Shifu an idea.

Shifu used food to train Po.

Po did sit-ups with dumplings.

He balanced bowls of soup on his head.

It was hard work. It made Po hungry.

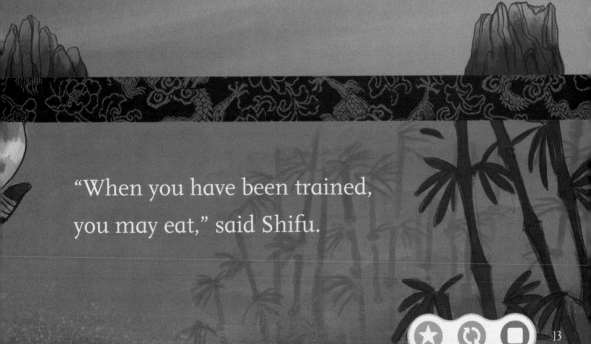

"When you have been trained,
you may eat," said Shifu.

Finally, Shifu put a bowl of dumplings in front of Po. This was the final test. All Po had to do was take a dumpling from Shifu.

Po was hungry. He used all the kung fu he had learned.

And he got it!

"You have done well, Panda," said Shifu.

"Done well? I've done awesome!" said Po.

"Yes," Shifu agreed. "You have done awesome."

And for the first time in a long time,

Shifu smiled.

tub

hug

run

hum

gut

wet

zen

leg

bed

red

r g l z t h b w

u e

b n g t m d

19

pl

sl

slug

claw

Guide to Kung Fu Diet

fr

cl

br

clam

frog

bran

plum

23

bamboo

tunnel

crocodile

piranha

crane

waterwheel

pagoda

waterfall

swamp